PUFFIN BOOKS

HAMMY
THE WONDER HAMSTER

'Goodnight now, Hammy,' Bethany said presently, putting him in the cage. Then she went to switch off her phone. But when she picked it up, she saw a text message on the screen that made her hand shake and her mouth drop open.

The text message would change her life. It read:

MY NAME IS HAMILTON. APPLE, PLEASE? THANKS.

Look out for more of Hammy's adventures ...

POPPY HARRIS

HAMMY THE WONDER HAMSTER

PUFFIN

PUFFIN BOOKS

Published by the Penguin Group
Penguin Books Ltd, 80 Strand, London WC2R ORL, England
Penguin Group (USA) Inc., 375 Hudson Street, New York, New York 10014, USA
Penguin Group (Canada), 90 Eglinton Avenue East, Suite 700, Toronto, Ontario, Canada M4P 2Y3
(a division of Pearson Penguin Canada Inc.)
Penguin Ireland, 25 St Stephen's Green, Dublin 2, Ireland (a division of Penguin Books Ltd)
Penguin Group (Australia), 250 Camberwell Road, Camberwell, Victoria 3124, Australia
(a division of Pearson Australia Group Pty Ltd)
Penguin Books India Pvt Ltd, 11 Community Centre, Panchsheel Park,
New Delhi – 110 017, India
Penguin Group (NZ), 67 Apollo Drive, Rosedale, North Shore 0632, New Zealand
(a division of Pearson New Zealand Ltd)
Penguin Books (South Africa) (Pty) Ltd, 24 Sturdee Avenue, Rosebank,
Johannesburg 2196, South Africa

Penguin Books Ltd, Registered Offices: 80 Strand, London WC2R ORL, England

puffinbooks.com

First published 2008
001

Text copyright © Poppy Harris, 2008
All rights reserved

The moral right of the author has been asserted

Set in 13.75/20.5pt Bembo
Typeset by Palimpsest Book Production Limited, Grangemouth, Stirlingshire
Made and printed in England by Clays Ltd, St Ives plc

British Library Cataloguing in Publication Data
A CIP catalogue record for this book is available from the British Library

ISBN: 978-0-141-38861-8

www.greenpenguin.co.uk

Penguin Books is committed to a sustainable future
for our business, our readers and our planet.
The book in your hands is made from paper
certified by the Forest Stewardship Council.

To Kayleigh

chapter 1

'That one,' said Bethany, 'please. The little golden and white one.'

Dolittle's Pet Shop smelt of sawdust and animals. On the crammed shelves were rows of packets of pet food, from little brown paper bags of budgie seed at one end to enormous cartons of biscuits for Great Danes at the other. Dog leads hung from the walls and a basket of squeaky toys lay on the counter. Everywhere was a steady *whirr-whirr-whirr* as hamsters ran and ran on their wheels.

Bethany had been watching the hamsters

for nearly half an hour, while her dad tried not to look bored and her younger brother, Sam, worked his way along the rows of rabbit cages. (He already had a rabbit, so he needed to make sure that none of the shop rabbits was as nice as his Bobby.) Bethany had observed every single hamster very carefully, couldn't make up her mind about which was her favourite and was about to start all over again when, in the cage nearest to her, something rustled.

There were two young hamsters in there, one pattering round on the wheel and the other standing up on its hind legs to drink from the water bottle, but Bethany could hear more rustling noises from the nest box. As she watched, a pink nose appeared. It twitched. Soon, she could see a small hamster face.

Bethany watched the hamster. There was something different about this one. She'd never seen such a bright, inquisitive look on an animal's face. The hamster darted to the feeding dish, picked up a sunflower seed and nibbled it. Then it stopped eating and put its head on one side, as if it had something to think about. Its eyes were bright, and in its soft, fluffed-up fur were patches as golden as honey.

'Hello,' said Bethany.

The hamster looked directly at her, twitching its nose. It was as if he smiled at her, and Bethany loved him.

'Dad,' she said. '*That* one.'

Dad stooped to peer into the cage. 'Isn't it a bit small?' he said. 'It's smaller than the others. It might not be very strong.'

'He's a young one, that's all,' said the woman behind the counter. 'That's why he's in there. If he were older, he'd be by himself. You can't put male hamsters in together like that when they start growing up, or they fight. He's already used to being handled, so he's very tame. A nice little hamster, that one. He has a bright face.'

'He's the right one,' said Bethany quietly. 'He's been waiting for me. He's *meant* to be mine. And it's my own money.'

'But, Bethany love, it looks as if it might be a runt,' said Dad. 'You can still think again.'

So Bethany did what she always did. She didn't argue, plead, sulk, cry or make a fuss. She just stood still, very calmly and quietly. If she had to stay there until closing time, she would. She would leave the shop with this hamster, or no hamster at all.

'It's just that you'd be so upset if it died,' said Dad. Bethany gave him a wide-eyed look, then put her hands behind her back and turned her steady gaze back to the hamster.

Half an hour later, she was in her bedroom. She had cleared the top of a little white chest of drawers so there was just enough room for a cage and boxes of hamster food. Beside her, a small cardboard box jiggled and rocked as the hamster inside scuffled about and poked his inquisitive, twitching nose through the holes. When Bethany was sure that the cage door would stay shut, the water bottle wouldn't fall off, and there was everything in there that a small hamster would need to make him feel at home, she opened the box very carefully, afraid that he might run away.

He didn't run away at all. He jumped straight into the cage and climbed up the bars, exploring. Bethany sat on her bed to watch him. The more she watched him the more she was surprised, and the more she was surprised, the more she was absolutely fascinated.

She had never owned a hamster before, but she knew a bit about them. Her friend Chloe had a hamster called Toffee, which was why Bethany had wanted one in the first place. Her mum and dad had said that she could have one if she proved how much she cared about it by paying for it herself, so she had saved up for a hamster, a cage, bowls and everything else needed to keep her pet happy. She had made sure to learn all she could about hamsters, too. This meant that she had a pretty good idea of how hamsters normally behaved, and this hamster wasn't normal at all.

For a start, there was the way his mouth twitched just as if he were about to sneeze, but he didn't. Then he made a face that was almost a smile, and another that was a sort of pout. It looked exactly as if he were trying to talk but couldn't quite manage it. Then he climbed into the wheel, took a little run, stopped, and turned round to see if it would go the other way. It didn't, so he stood on his hind legs, stretched up to the screw holding the wheel to the cage, and wiggled it with his forepaws. Bethany giggled. Of course, he was only exploring, but he looked like a mechanic checking a car.

The feeling that she was being watched made Bethany turn round. Sam was peeping round the door.

'You're supposed to knock,' said Bethany.

Sam knocked, then came straight in without waiting for an answer and bent to look into the cage.

'Can I see Hammy?' he asked.

'He's not called Hammy,' said Bethany, though she wasn't sure yet what he was called. Chloe's hamster was Toffee, so she'd thought of calling hers Choccie, or Caramel, or even Peanut, but none of these suited him. It seemed unkind to call him after something to eat. Sam had become strangely quiet. 'But all hamsters are called Hammy, aren't they?' he said. 'Even if they're called something else as well.'

He stuffed his hand into his pocket, drew out a very battered home-made card, and gave it to her. Under a drawing of a hamster, he had written with coloured felt pens: *Welcome home, Hammy*.

'Oh!' said Bethany. 'Thank you!' It was surprisingly sweet of him, and she hoped she hadn't hurt his feelings.

'Hammy could be short for something,' she said, propping up the card against one side of the cage.

'Ham sandwich?' suggested Sam, but at that moment Mum called them both for tea.

'I'll be down in a minute,' shouted Bethany.

Sam ran down the stairs, but Bethany stopped to have one more minute with her hamster. When he'd finished playing with the wheel the hamster took a good look at the fastening on the door, inspecting it from above, below and each side as if he were determined to know how it worked. Then he turned his attention to the scraps of newspaper on the cage floor, scratching at them with his claws and picking up fragments in his teeth.

'Are you making yourself a nest?' Bethany said. That was what Toffee would have done, dragging torn shreds of paper to the nest box, and for a moment it looked as if this hamster would do the same – only he didn't. She leant forward to watch more closely. The hamster rearranged the pieces on the floor of the cage, lining them up, running round them to see what they looked like and moving them about. By the time Mum called again, he had put together half a crossword and most of the Sudoku.

Bethany was still thinking about her hamster as she washed and went downstairs.

'How's your hamster settling in?' asked Mum as she spooned spaghetti Bolognese on to plates.

'He's brilliant!' said Bethany, and felt the smile spreading across her face when she thought about him. 'He's really clever. I mean, *really*. He tried out the wheel and I think he wanted it to go the other way, because he stood on his hind legs and twiddled the screw. And he looks at everything very carefully, as if he wants to see how it works.'

'He's making an escape plan,' said Sam.

'Don't give him a screwdriver, whatever you do,' said Dad.

Bethany ignored the teasing. 'His mouth twitches,' she said. 'Not just ordinary twitches – it looks as if he wants to talk, he sort of smiles, and –'

There was a snort and a splutter from Sam.

'Sam!' said Mum.

'Smiley hamster!' gasped Sam. He put on a beaming wide-eyed smile, tucked his lower lip under his front teeth, crossed his eyes, and folded over, braying with laughter. 'Smiley Hammy!'

'But he —' said Bethany.

'Talking ha-ham-ham—' began Sam, and was laughing too much to say anything else.

'That's enough,' said Mum, and Bethany, with a glance at Sam's shaking shoulders, decided Mum was right. That was more than enough. She'd be very careful what she said about her hamster now, especially if Sam were there.

'Has he got a name yet?' asked Dad.

Bethany put down her knife and fork and glared at Sam before he could say 'Ham Sandwich'. 'Not yet,' she said. 'I'm still thinking.'

Upstairs in his cage, Hammy the Hamster was thinking about his name too. At the same time, he'd worked out all the crossword answers in his head and started on the Sudoku.

Bethany was right about her hamster. He was completely unlike any other hamster ever, and there was a reason for that, but not even he fully understood what it was. To find that out, you need to know what had happened about a week earlier in a scientific lab at the nearest university. And you need to know about a young man – thin, with messy hair that wouldn't lie flat, square glasses and clothes that always looked too big for him – called Tim Taverner.

chapter 2

Tim Taverner had been the most brilliant science student at the university. He was so brilliant that while still a young man he had passed the difficult exams, the even more difficult exams and the almost impossible exams, so that the university was running out of letters to put after his name. He had stayed at the university, teaching other students while working on more projects of his own. He was particularly interested in two things – computers and artificial intelligence.

He didn't talk much about the work he was doing. That was because he wasn't supposed to be doing it at all. Artificial intelligence was a dangerous thing. Tim should have had twenty different licences to do those projects. He only had three, and two of those were out of date. Also, he should have had two supervisors to observe what he was doing and, if necessary, tell him to stop it. Tim had no supervisors at all, and a lot of his work was strictly against the law.

For about half of each week, Tim taught students how to teach computers to speak two hundred different languages, compose music, design aeroplanes and solve puzzles. For the other half, he worked in a lab trying to get the most possible information and intelligence into the tiniest possible microchip – or, as he called it, a microspeck.

The microspeck project was all going very well, and Tim was more and more excited about it. He would go into the lab as early as he could and stay as late as he could. Usually, he would give his morning lectures first, then hurry to the canteen to buy soup or a sandwich for lunch. On this particular Friday, he chose an apple and a salad baguette with sesame seeds on the top, and rushed back to his desk to eat them while he worked. All afternoon he made notes, scribbled down figures, programmed and reprogrammed, processed information and calculated, darting from the screen to the safe and from the safe to the electron microscope. Occasionally, he remembered to take a bite out of his sandwich. This meant that there were smears of margarine and tomato-coloured splodges on his notes but, as most of them ended up in the bin, it didn't matter. Finally, when he had worked so long and so frantically that the words and figures were mixed up in his mind, he swept the remaining sandwich crumbs into the bin, put on his jacket and locked up the lab. He spent the weekend at a conference about how to teach computers to make weather forecasts, then gave lectures all Monday, so it was Tuesday when he went back to the lab. Full of new ideas, he unlocked the safe and took out the vacuum bag where he kept the microspeck.

It was empty.

He stared, peered into the bag, shook it upside down and turned it inside out. He inspected the corners, hoping that the microspeck might have fallen into one and got stuck. It was no good.

He tried to remember all he had done on Friday evening. He had put the microspeck into the vacuum bag as he always did, hadn't he? Or had he, in a careless moment, put the bag away without checking and double-checking to make sure the microspeck was really in there? Had he put the bag away empty? The more he thought of it, the more he realized, with sweat breaking out on his forehead and his hands trembling, that this was exactly what he had done. He dashed to his desk – it might still be on there – but the desk was neat and clean.

Think, Tim, he told himself. *Take a deep breath. What did you do last thing on Friday?*

He remembered tidying away the rubbish on Friday night. Then he covered his face with his hands, made a sound that was half a groan and half a growl, and dashed to the waste-paper basket. He knew he'd swept the sandwich crumbs into it, along with some notes, his apple core, the newspaper and a paper aeroplane he'd been making because it helped him to think. There was no doubt about it. The microspeck had been cleared away with the rubbish and swept into the waste-paper basket. It had, of course, been emptied twice since Friday. All the same, he tipped it up, shook it, smacked it and shook it again, just in case anything dropped out, and looked into its corners with a magnifying lens to see if anything had got stuck to the side. But the cleaners did their work very thoroughly, and there wasn't a trace of anything at all.

He examined the surface of his desk and moved the computer in case the microspeck had rolled underneath, but nothing lay there, not even a speck of dust. On his hands and knees, he examined the carpet through the magnifying lens. It was clean and speckless.

There was still hope. Tim often worked late, and knew what time the cleaners would arrive. He settled down for a long wait.

The time dragged. The hands on the clock scarcely moved. Eventually, at seven o'clock, he heard the welcome sound of mops rattling in buckets and vacuum cleaners purring in the corridors. The door opened, and before him stood a short, curly-haired, kind-faced woman in a pink overall. The vacuum cleaner sat beside her like a well-trained dog, and she carried a basket of dusters and polish.

'I'll not get in your way, Dr Taverner,' she said cheerfully.

'Oh – Mary –' said Tim, out of breath with anxiety – 'I need to ask you about something – er – important. *Very* important. Did you do the cleaning in here on Friday?'

'Yes, I did, Dr Taverner,' she said, looking worried. 'I hope there's nothing the matter?'

'Oh, no – nothing, nothing at all,' he said quickly. 'Only, I was wondering – can you tell me –' the next words came out in a rush – 'can you tell me what happens to the rubbish from the waste-paper baskets?'

'What a question!' she said. Now she came to look at him, Dr Taverner didn't seem at all well. She felt sorry for him and spoke reassuringly, as if he were a small boy. 'All the paper has to be shredded, then most of the cleaners put all the rubbish out for the binmen. But not me.' She lowered her voice as if letting him in on a guilty secret. 'I hate waste. I take the shredded paper to my daughter. She works in a pet shop and the paper comes in very useful for putting in cages, for bedding and that. For the hamsters.'

Tim leapt to his feet, flung his arms round Mary, and hugged her so hard that she squeaked.

'Mary!' he cried. 'You are wonderful! Which pet shop is it?'

Dolittle's Pet Shop had shut long before Tim got there, so he had to wait until the next day to talk to them. By then it was four days since a certain young hamster had found some shredded paper and the remains of a paper aeroplane that tasted deliciously of apple. He had a feeling that something got stuck in his pouch when he was eating, but by then he was already thinking of apples and aeroplanes.

chapter 3

While Bethany finished her tea, the hamster was still thinking about his name. *A hamster*, he thought, *should be allowed to choose a name for himself.* Then he'd have to let Bethany know what it was. What could 'Hammy' be short for?

Tim Taverner had programmed the microchip with an encyclopaedia or two and a few dictionaries. It was easy for Hammy to run through a list of things beginning with 'Ham'.

Hamilton – that was nice. There was a play about a prince called Hamlet, but he was rather a sad prince and died at the end. No, he wouldn't be Hamlet. Hammerhead shark? Definitely not. Then there was Hammurabi. He was a king, but not a very nice one. Now he came to think of it, 'Hamilton' had a very pleasant sound to it. It was the name of a place in Scotland, a football team, and some Very Important People. He could be Hamilton the Handsome, or Hamilton the Hero. Yes. Hammy was short for 'Hamilton'.

'May I leave the table?' asked Bethany when she'd hardly swallowed her last mouthful.

'If you're quite sure you've had enough to eat,' said Mum.

Bethany didn't care whether she'd had enough or not. She only wanted to get back to her hamster. As she ran into her bedroom, the door banged behind her and he bolted for the safety of his nest box. Presently, he popped his head over the edge.

'Sorry, Hammy,' she said. 'I didn't mean to frighten you.'

He looked at her, gave a little shrug as if to say that it didn't matter, and scampered to the middle of the cage. The newspaper he had been playing with had been roughly patched together like a jigsaw. At that moment, Bethany remembered something her friend Chloe had told her – newspaper shouldn't be given to hamsters. It was something to do with the print not being good for them if they tried to eat it. She reached into the cage to take it out, and suddenly was very puzzled, twice.

The first puzzling thing was this – maybe any hamster might leave the scraps of paper lined up like that, but surely no other hamster would get all the pieces in the right order? The second was that, when she reached into the cage to take the newspaper out, the hamster firmly sat down on it and refused to move. His eyes looked fierce with indignation.

Perhaps she'd better leave him alone. She shut the door. 'Just don't eat the crossword,' she said. 'It might upset your tummy.'

She could have called her parents, or Sam, to come and see what he'd done – but when you don't believe your own eyes, how can you expect anyone else to believe them? What she really wanted to do was to get him out of the cage to play, but there was the awkward question of maths homework to do first. She'd have to do it now, as quickly as possible, to get it out of the way and have the rest of the evening to play with her hamster. Bethany sat down at her desk.

She worked out the easy questions first, went back to the ones that were too difficult, and, finally, frowned and struggled over the one she couldn't do at all. Bethany always found maths difficult and had just started doing percentages. She didn't understand them, so the question about 11 per cent of £14.00 left her completely confused, and the more she tried to make sense of it, the more confusing it became. When she still couldn't do it she decided that she'd understand it better after a little break, so she opened the cage door and lifted the hamster on to her hand.

Hamilton was very glad about this. He'd been getting bored. Having put the Sudoku back together again, he'd completed it in his head and tried to scratch in the answers, but the paper kept crumpling up and tearing. Then he'd tried to say 'Bethany', but found his mouth couldn't make the right sounds. He had a go at saying 'Hamilton', then 'Hammy', but that was a lot harder than working out Sudoku in his head. The microchip in his cheek meant that he understood any language, including animal languages, and could read as many alphabets as Tim had crammed into the memory, but a hamster mouth isn't much good at speaking human languages, so Hamilton's attempts to speak English left him cross and frustrated. Searching for something else to do, he had explored every corner of his cage and had already worked out how to open the catch and let himself out before Bethany opened the door.

Bethany sat her new hamster in the palm of one hand and thought that he looked like a fluffy pom-pom, but an intelligent fluffy pom-pom. She stroked his head very gently with one finger. Not for the first time, she was telling herself that he was really, truly hers. She took in every detail of his soft fur, his pink ears, his delicate colour and the way his nose twitched. His dark eyes were bright, as if he were looking forward to something.

'My hamster,' she whispered. 'Really mine.

I can't believe it. I'm glad I saved up and bought you myself because it makes you even more mine, doesn't it, little Hammy? That name will do for now, until you have a proper one. You're the best hamster in the world!'

This puzzled Hamilton a bit. Was he really that special? But more than anything else, he felt warmly and wonderfully happy. Bethany had bought him and thought the world of him, and what could be better than that?

'Do you like your cage?' she asked softly. 'This is your home.'

He very much wanted to say, 'It's a very nice cage, thank you, and I like you too,' but it was no good trying. Instead, he observed her face with great care. Hair – dark brown, a little past her shoulders. Something gold was growing on her head – oh, that was a hairband. Eyes – greeny-brown. She was still wearing her school sweater, which looked worth exploring, so he ran up her sleeve, popped out at her collar and scrambled on to her shoulder. His whiskers tickled her neck.

Bethany laughed, picked him up and was about to put him on the floor when she remembered that she was supposed to put something over the carpet first. She was pretty sure that her new Hammy was much too well-behaved to poo and pee on carpets, but she'd better not risk it. It would have to be newspaper again. She put what was left of the paper on her desk, gently placed him on it, and told him not to eat it. Then she looked down at her homework.

Hamilton loved newspapers! He wouldn't dream of wasting one by eating it! While Bethany spread her books on the desk beside him he read all about the prime minister's visit to Preston, the price of petrol in Poland and a woman who believed that carrots were intelligent. It was all very interesting but there weren't any puzzles on that page, so he scrabbled the edge of the page to lift it up and burrowed underneath. He could see an article about helicopters, which was really exciting. From the corner of her eye, Bethany saw something move.

'Hammy?' she said. For one terrible moment, she didn't know where he was – then she saw the bulge moving about in the newspaper.

'Hammy!' she cried, and lifted the page to pick him up, but Hamilton, who had just got to the best bit, jumped down again and ran straight back to his place. Bethany watched the way his head moved from left to right. He looked exactly as if he were reading.

He was a fast reader, and had soon finished with the newspaper. Now, he was curious to know what Bethany was doing, so he scratched at her shoe till she looked down, laughed, and put him on her desk. She wanted to play with him, but instead she gave herself a little shake and looked down again at her homework. She wasn't supposed to use her calculator to do this *and* she was supposed to show how she worked out the answer.

'But that's the trouble!' she said aloud to Hammy. 'If I knew how to work out the answer, I would have done it by now!'

Hamilton ran over her hand and on to her book to see what she was doing. He made another great effort to speak because he wanted very much to tell her that 11 per cent of £14.00 was £1.54, but the words were too difficult to pronounce. Perhaps he could scratch it on the page – he began to make claw marks. *One, decimal point –*

'Hammy!' cried Bethany, picking him up again. 'Are you playing with the paper?' She kissed him and put him back down. Hamilton sighed deeply. Humans were supposed to be the most intelligent species on earth, so why didn't this one understand what he was trying to tell her?

That was when he noticed the calculator. He had no idea *how* he knew what a calculator was, but of course he *did* know. He pressed all the right keys to show her the answer, but she was looking for an eraser and didn't see him. Finally, she decided that the only thing to do was to ask Dad for help, and took her hamster downstairs with her.

Dad was watching a quiz programme. He sat down at the table with Bethany and explained about percentages, while Hamilton took his place on the armchair, watched the quiz, and wondered why all the questions were too easy. With a bit of help and explanation, Bethany had soon worked out that the answer to the question was £1.54, then she asked:

'Dad?'

'Yes, love?' said Dad.

'It's about my Hammy,' she said, and didn't know how to go on. She wanted to tell Dad about the patched-up puzzles and the way Hammy had seemed to be reading, but perhaps she should be careful. Dad might think she was just being silly. Worse, he might think there was something wrong with her beautiful new hamster and want to take him back to the shop.

'What about him?' asked Dad. He turned to stroke Hamilton's golden head with a finger, and laughed. 'Look at him! He looks as if he's watching the telly.'

'I mean ...' She began to wish she hadn't started. It wouldn't be easy to explain this. 'He seems to be very intelligent – I mean, more than you would expect for a hamster.'

''Course he is, love,' he said, and hugged her. 'The cleverest hamster in the world.'

Bethany sighed. She decided to leave it at that. Dad wouldn't understand. Not even Chloe would understand, and if she did she might be jealous because Toffee wasn't clever. She went back to her room, put her hamster in his cage and, tidying up her school books, picked up her calculator. Standing out on the screen, as clearly as could be, was '£1.54'.

Bethany knew very well that she hadn't worked it out. She hadn't touched the calculator. The hamster was running happily in his wheel.

'Hammy?' she said. But he simply went on running, only stopping to drink from his bottle or eat a sunflower seed. He looked just like Toffee or any other hamster. Thinking of Toffee reminded her that she hadn't told Chloe about her hamster yet. Bethany picked up her mobile phone and keyed a text – GT MY HMSTR! YAY! – then sent it to Chloe with a photograph.

It would be nice to hold him once more before she got ready for bed. She took him out and let him run from one hand to the other, his little paws tickling her palms, then, while she packed her school bags, put him down for a moment beside her phone.

'Goodnight now, Hammy,' she said presently, putting him in the cage, then she went to switch off her phone. But when she picked it up, she saw a text message on the screen that made her hand shake and her mouth drop open.

The text message would change her life. It read:

MY NAME IS HAMILTON. APPLE, PLEASE? THANKS.

At that moment, Tim Taverner was at home in the room he used as a bedroom, a study, a workshop and a laboratory. He'd have to make a tracking device. With a microchip detector powerful and accurate enough, he should be able to find the microspeck and get it back. He would be teaching all the next day, but at the very first chance he would go down to Dolittle's Pet Shop.

chapter 4

Long after Bethany was supposed to be in bed, she sat up, hugging her dressing gown round her and feeding slices of apple to Hamilton. She had written down sums for him and he had tapped out the answers on the text keys. Then she had given him a few more which were so hard she couldn't work them out herself, which meant she couldn't be sure if his answers were right or not (but they looked more or less right to her). She had asked him if he knew any other languages and he had tapped out JE COMPRENDS

FRANCAIS, ICH VERSTEHE DEUTSCH and I SPEAK RABBIT. Then he had listed as many of his other languages as he could, but the text keys only did the English alphabet so he couldn't answer in Russian, Japanese or Arabic. Finally, she put the phone on her bed and Hamilton on her hand.

'How do you know all this?' she asked.

Hamilton shrugged. DON'T KNOW, he tapped out.

'Most hamsters aren't as clever as you,' she said, stroking him with a finger.

Hamilton lowered his head shyly, a little to one side. He looked pleased, but a bit embarrassed.

'But where do you get all this from?' she asked. 'I mean, being able to think and calculate, and learn things?'

He spread his paws and shook his head. He had no idea where his intelligence came from.

38

'But – but you are a real hamster, aren't you?' she said.

He nodded earnestly and, just to prove that he was as hamster as a hamster could be, stretched out his paws to his cage. Bethany placed him in it, and he picked up a sunflower seed and ate it. He stored another one in his pouch for later, then jumped on to his wheel and ran until it whirred so fast that his paws looked like eight instead of four. Finally, he jumped off and rubbed his face against her hand.

All this made two things very clear to Bethany. One was that Hamilton, though he was wonderfully, amazingly intelligent, was a normal hamster in every other way. He still needed to eat, sleep and run as all hamsters ate, slept and ran. He needed to be looked after, just like any other pet.

The other thing she realized was that it would be best, for the moment, to keep his intelligence a secret. If other people knew how clever he was, he was sure to be taken away. He'd probably be kept in a lab somewhere, and he wouldn't like that.

'Hamilton,' she said. He put his head on one side and looked at her, washing his paws. 'Hamilton Hammy, you're a very, *very* clever hamster. But if other people know how clever you are they might try to take you away from me. So, when other people are here, you must behave like any ordinary hamster, just like the ones in the pet shop. Do you understand that?'

He thought, nodded, and jumped on to her phone. WHAT IF I FORGET HOW THEY BEHAVE? he tapped out.

'I don't think you will,' said Bethany, and had an idea. 'I'll get Chloe to bring Toffee here. He's an ordinary hamster. You can watch him.'

★

Tim Taverner didn't know much about hamsters, but it didn't take him long to work out that even if the microspeck had been swallowed by a hamster, he'd still be able to get it back. Whatever went into a hamster's mouth was sure to come out, sooner or later, at the other end. He felt a lot calmer when he'd worked this out. All he had to do now was to take his tracking device down to Dolittle's Pet Shop.

Oh, bother, he thought. *It won't be that easy.* If he wandered about with a tracking device that bleeped when it came near the microspeck, everyone would notice. And if anybody asked him what he was doing, he couldn't very well say he was looking for hamster poo – and not just any old hamster poo but a Very Important Poo.

Perhaps he could say he was doing a very important project for the government about hamster poo. No, they wouldn't believe it.

And if they did, it might be worse. They might give him whole wheelbarrows full of it to take home.

Think, Tim, he told himself. *Think*. He asked himself questions and gave himself the answers.

1. Who could go into a pet shop and look around anywhere, absolutely anywhere, with nobody minding?
– *A pet shop inspector*, he told himself.

2. How can I persuade them that I'm a pet shop inspector?
– *Find out what one looks like.*

He turned to the computer and tapped into the search engine: PET SHOP INSPECTORS. Up popped a lot of brightly coloured adverts telling him where he could buy pedigree gerbils, sparkly dog collars and budgie mirrors. Finally, after a lot of searching and clicking, he found that to be an inspector he would need a suit (not too smart), a white coat (he had lots of those), a clipboard and an identity badge (he could fake one of those).

Nobody must know who he really was, so of course he wouldn't use his own name. And, just in case he met anyone he knew, he'd better disguise himself.

Bethany and Chloe had known each other as long as they could remember, and lived in the same street. They were so much the same size and height that people sometimes forgot who was who, and just called Bethany 'the dark one' and Chloe 'the blonde one'. If they knew them a bit better, they said Bethany was the quiet one and Chloe was the chatterbox.

Bethany and Chloe sat on Bethany's bed, each holding a cage with a hamster inside.

Toffee was a soft brown colour, and bigger than Hamilton. Of course, Chloe had said 'He's *lovely*!' about Hamilton, and she really meant it, but secretly she thought that Toffee was much nicer. And, of course, Bethany thought Hamilton was much nicer than Toffee, and she *knew* he was much cleverer, but she was too polite to say so.

Bethany and Chloe both knew that two male hamsters should not be put together, or they'd fight. That was why they had agreed that Toffee and Hamilton mustn't get too close to each other.

Toffee wasn't much of a fighter. His favourite things were eating, sleeping and making nests so he could do some more sleeping. Even so, he glared at Hamilton.

'Can I hold your Hammy?' asked Chloe.

''Course you can,' said Bethany.

Chloe opened Hamilton's cage and lifted him out. 'Aah!' she said as she held him in the palm of her hand and stroked his head. 'Hello, little Hammy!'

Toffee was not at all pleased about this. Chloe was *his*. No cheeky little newcomer had the right to sit on her hand, and he clutched the bars of his cage like a prisoner, baring his teeth at Hamilton. The girls couldn't understand what they said to each other in Hamster, which was just as well.

'Hey, you! Titch!' said Toffee. 'That's my Chloe you're sitting on!'

Hamilton shrugged. 'Is that a problem?' he asked. 'She picked me up. But, if you like ...'

He jumped from Chloe's hand into Bethany's lap. ('Aah!' said both the girls.) From here, he ran to Toffee's cage and sat a few centimetres from it, looking at Toffee through the bars.

'Pleased to meet you!' he said.

'You come any nearer and I'll sort you,' warned Toffee.

Hamilton scratched his head. His hamster instincts told him that he and Toffee should fight, but his intelligence told him there was no good reason for it.

'I know we're supposed to fight,' he said, 'but I don't know why.'

'Get away!' said Toffee (but he didn't know why either). 'You stay out of my cage!'

'No problem!' said Hamilton, who was already very fond of his own cage. He'd got the bed just the way he liked it, and he'd carried out a bit of light engineering on the wheel to give it three gears. 'And I suppose you'll stay out of mine?'

'Cheeky little kid,' growled Toffee. 'I'll fight you.'

'Done much fighting, have you?' asked Hamilton, washing his paws.

'Er . . .' said Toffee. He hadn't, but he didn't want to say so.

'Tell you what,' said Hamilton, 'I won't fight you and you won't fight me. Is that a deal?'

'Er . . . all right,' said Toffee, who was getting puzzled.

'We could even be friends,' said Hamilton.

'What?' said Toffee, who couldn't understand what Hamilton was talking about.

'Friends,' said Hamilton, 'like my Bethany and your Chloe.'

'What?' said Toffee again. He didn't want to be like Bethany and Chloe, who talked and laughed a lot and sometimes wore pink. 'You're daft, you.'

'You're welcome. My name's Hamilton, but you can call me Hammy.' A short name would be easier for Toffee to remember.

While the hamsters were getting to know each other, Bethany and Chloe had been talking about what to do next. Chloe wanted to go down to Dolittle's to buy some more hamster food for Toffee, and Bethany said she'd go too. She was putting Hamilton in his cage when she felt his claw tighten round her finger, as if he wanted to tell her something.

She looked down, and he nodded towards her phone. She glanced over her shoulder to see if Chloe was watching, but Chloe was putting on her coat and had her back to them. Bethany held the phone in front of Hamilton.

ME 2? he tapped in, and looked hopefully up at her. He was watching her with his head on one side and his eyes were like the eyes of a puppy pleading for a walk.

Chloe was now talking to Toffee. Quickly, Bethany opened her shoulder bag (a purple one with white kittens on it) and Hamilton jumped in. Bethany put a finger to her lips to make it clear to him that nobody, not even Chloe, must know he was in there.

'I'll leave Toffee here, if that's all right,' said Chloe. 'Bye-bye, Toffee, be good. Come on, Bethany, they'll be closing soon.'

chapter 5

'Can I help you, sir?' asked the lady behind the counter at Dolittle's Pet Shop. Her name was Theresa Nelson. She had only worked there for six months, and enjoyed it very much. She particularly liked to talk to the children who came in to buy food and toys for their pets. She knew all the regular customers by now, and even remembered the names of their animals, but she didn't know the man standing at the counter today. His hair was grey at the front and black at the back, and perhaps he had dandruff because there was a light powdering of something white on the shoulder of his jacket. She tried not to stare at his moustache, which looked oddly lopsided. Maybe he had trimmed it in a bad light. He carried a clipboard in his hand and a white coat over his arm.

'I'm the inspector,' said Tim Taverner. 'Charles Newton.' He showed her the fake identity pass he had made. (He had enjoyed making that badge and was really quite proud of it.)

Charles Newton
Quality Team Pet Inspection Executive
QTPIE

Theresa turned the badge to the light to take a good look at it. It seemed genuine. Nobody had told her that an inspector would be calling, but maybe that was the idea — it was one of those surprise inspections, so that you don't have time to sort everything out and have a good clean first. There was nobody else in the shop to ask about it, and Theresa knew that the all the pets were well cared for. Everything was clean, tidy and organized. The inspector was welcome to do all the inspecting he liked.

'Go ahead,' she said. 'Where would you like to start?'

Tim Taverner nearly said 'Hamster poo' because that's what he was thinking about, but he stopped himself in time.

'Rubbish!' he announced.

'I beg your pardon?' said Theresa.

'I need to see the rubbish bins,' he said. 'Where are they?'

Theresa could understand that an inspector would need to see that the rubbish was safely and cleanly disposed of. She led him out to the little courtyard at the back of the shop.

'Dustbins are here, sir,' she said. 'All the

rubbish goes into black plastic bags before it goes in the dustbins. We always wear plastic gloves for cleaning the cages and we always wash our hands after handling animals. Would you like to see the washroom?'

'Rubbish bins first,' said Tim, trying very hard to be patient. He was getting excited at the thought of finding the microspeck, and didn't want to be kept from those bins any longer.

'You'll need protective gloves, sir,' she said. 'The only ones we've got are purple, I'm afraid.' Tim was so keen that he almost snatched them from her.

A bell rang as the shop door opened.

'Excuse me,' she said, 'I have customers.'

'Oh, yes, you go and serve your customers – off you go!' said Tim, hoping this was the sort of thing a real inspector would say. He couldn't wait to get her out of the way.

While Theresa was in the shop selling poop scoops and cat mats, Tim took out his tracking device (it looked very like a mobile phone) and scanned the dustbins. But the device stayed silent. If he'd been near the microspeck, the light on the display would have glowed and there would have been a faint bleep – he had turned down the volume in case people noticed and wondered what he was doing. He ran the scanner up and down the sides of the bins.

Nothing bleeped. Nothing glowed. He tried again – then it occurred to him that, of course, these dustbins were made of metal. He had been in such a hurry to make his tracking device that he hadn't bothered to make sure it could detect anything through a metal dustbin. Drawing on the purple gloves Theresa had given him, and wrinkling up his nose, he lifted out a black bin liner.

The smell wasn't really that bad, but it was enough to make him look away over his shoulder and hold the bin bag as far from his nose as possible, as if it might bite him. Holding the tracker in the other hand, he turned his head just enough to see what he was doing.

Theresa glanced out of the window and saw the inspector lifting out each bag of rubbish in turn and running a scanner over it. He seemed to be doing the job very thoroughly, even though he clearly wasn't enjoying it. These inspectors must take their job very seriously.

Tim slammed the bin lids back on with a clatter. After all that, there wasn't a trace of the microspeck. He'd searched through all those smelly bin bags for nothing.

He cheered up at once when he thought that, if the microspeck wasn't in the rubbish, it must still be somewhere in the shop! Perhaps it was lying in the bottom of a cage somewhere! That must be it. He wasn't beaten yet. Hoping he didn't smell too bad and feeling in need of a good wash, he walked back into the shop.

'Thank you,' he said to Theresa. In spite of being hot, bothered and untidy, he still tried very hard to sound like an inspector. 'I'd like to see the washroom now, please.'

'Certainly,' said Theresa. 'It's the door on your right.'

'Thank you,' said Tim, and sneezed. Either the dust from the bins or the talcum powder in his hair must have got up his nose.

'Bless you!' said Theresa.

Tim straightened his shoulders and strode to the washroom. He was used to laboratories where every tap and every sink was scrubbed until it gleamed. At the lab, everything, including the toilets, had to be as clean as an operating theatre. He guessed that a pet shop washroom would be shabby and a bit scruffy, but it would have to do.

He pushed open the washroom door and blinked several times. This was Theresa's washroom and she was very proud of it. She liked to keep everything sparkling, spotless, mauve and smelling of lavender. The curtains, carpet, towels and all the frilly things – and there were a lot of frilly things – were mauve. There was lavender soap, as well as lavender air freshener, and a little box of mauve tissues. A mauve loo brush stood in a mauve holder.

Tim looked in the mirror and was horrified to see that his artificial moustache was hanging sideways and about to fall off. He tidied himself up as well as he could, eased his moustache back into place, checked that the tracking device in his pocket was still switched on, and returned to the shop smelling very sweetly of lavender.

Two girls, one dark and one blonde, had come into the shop while he was getting

washed. Tim ignored them. He was only
interested in the hamsters, and began to run
the tracker along the hamster cages, one by
one. By this time he was sure that the
microspeck must be in one of them, maybe
stuck in a corner that hadn't been properly
cleaned. Peering through the bars as closely
as he could without getting his nose bitten,
he kept the tracking device half-hidden
in his hand – but to his great disappointment,
there was still no bleep and no glowing
light.

The two girls were picking up pet toys –
rubber bones and catnip mice – and giggling
about them. The blonde one said, 'Listen to
this, Bethany,' and squeezed a rubber mouse
so that it squeaked – *ee-ee-ee!*. Tim frowned.
He was trying to listen for the bleep, and
their silly chat and laughter wasn't helping.
Drawing himself up to his full height, he
glared down at them, but they weren't

looking. He wished they'd just buy something and go.

On the way to the pet shop Hamilton had enjoyed his ride in Bethany's bag enormously. He had explored the bag, tasted it (nice!), chewed a corner of an old bus ticket and a pencil, then yawned, curled up, and fallen asleep. He was woken by two things. One was the *ee-ee-ee!* from the rubber mouse. The other was a strange buzzing feeling in his right cheek pouch.

He sat up and scrabbled at his cheek. It tingled. It didn't hurt, but there was an uncomfortable tugging sensation that made his head twitch to one side. Hamilton had no idea what it meant, but he knew he didn't like it a bit. He rubbed his cheek against Bethany's bag to see if that made it stop.

Tim Taverner gave a little squeak and a jump. Theresa looked up in alarm, wondering if he'd poked his finger through the bars of a cage and been bitten. *Serve him right*, she thought.

'Are you all right, sir?' she asked.

'Yes!' said Tim, a bit crossly. He needed to concentrate. His heart was beating wildly. On the tracking device, the light glowed. Faintly, it beeped. He scanned the cages again, but the signal failed, and it was only when he turned away from them that the light glowed and the signal bleeped again. Could the microspeck be on the floor?

Hamilton stopped rubbing his face against the inside of Bethany's bag because it wasn't doing any good. The tingling and twitching went on, so he tried to run away from it. There wasn't much room to run anywhere in a shoulder bag but, in the very second he ran behind Bethany's mobile phone, the buzzing and tugging stopped abruptly. He stayed there, curled up behind Bethany's phone, keeping very still. As long as he stayed there, nothing buzzed in his cheek.

Tim Taverner, completely puzzled, looked at the tracker device. He'd lost the signal. He tapped sharply at it to see if it was still working, then bit his nails. The microspeck was definitely in here somewhere. There *had* been a signal. It seemed to be strongest just around the spot where those two girls were standing, and he scowled. They were in his way. He wished they'd just go home. It didn't help at all that, at that moment, every hamster in the shop decided to climb on to its wheel and go for a run. All that whirring made it hard to concentrate, but he tried to work things out. If the microspeck had been in the hamster bedding, it should now be in the rubbish, but it wasn't. *What if it was still inside a hamster?* But it couldn't be, surely? Not after all this time?

In the bag, Bethany's phone rang. Hamilton

jumped in surprise. Bethany took out the phone. On the tracking device in Tim's hand the signal returned, strong and clear. Hamilton's pouch tingled and twitched again.

chapter 6

Shaking with excitement, Tim looked about.
Stay there, my little microspeck, he thought. *I'm
here. I'm coming to find you.* The microspeck's
signal was definitely coming from somewhere
near that dark-haired girl. It must be very
close to her. Oh, why couldn't she just get
out of the way? The microspeck might be
jammed in the floorboards at her feet! He
scowled at her again, but she had turned the
other way to talk into her phone, and wasn't
looking.

'Excuse me,' he muttered, pushing past

her as he tried to find the source of the signal.

'I'm just going outside, Chloe,' said Bethany. 'It's too noisy in here with all those wheels spinning.'

She frowned at the man who had just pushed past her and went outside. It was just good luck that she stood beside a large metal litter bin that blocked Tim's signal completely, but of course Tim didn't realize this. He only knew that he was left again without a microspeck, without a signal and without a clue. But there *had* been a signal!

Bethany came in again, dropping her phone into her bag. Hamilton curled up behind it.

'That was my mum,' she said to Chloe. 'She's coming down in five minutes, so we can have a lift home.'

'Cool,' said Chloe, and went to the

counter to buy hamster food. Theresa, who remembered her, smiled warmly at her.

'How's Toffee?' she asked.

'He's fine, thanks,' said Chloe, very pleased to be asked.

Theresa turned to Bethany. 'And how's your new hamster?' she asked.

Tim dropped the tracking device and scrabbled on the floor for it.

Bethany beamed. 'He's fine, thank you,' she said. 'He's really sweet, I love him to bits.'

'Has he settled in?' asked Theresa.

'Oh, yes,' said Bethany. 'Straight away.'

'We'd better wait outside for your mum,' said Chloe.

Tim stared after them as they left. The signal had come from near them, and they both owned hamsters – in fact, one of them had a *new* hamster, bought from this shop! Could the microspeck be something to do with this girl's hamster? And which

girl was it – the dark one or the blonde
one?

'Sir?' said Theresa.

'What?' he snapped, and then remembered
his manners. 'I mean ... er ...'

'Do you want to inspect the food supplies?'
she asked helpfully. 'And the cleaning records?
And the health records? We clean out every
cage, every single morning.'

He could see the girls outside, chatting
as they waited for their lift home. He mustn't
lose sight of them, but he was still pretending
to be an inspector. He peered over the rows
of hamster food and tried to sound as if he
knew what he was talking about.

'Yes – very healthy, very good, very well
displayed,' he said. 'Good balanced diet, that's
what I like to see. Very good. Well done.
That's all I need to see.'

'Then – have we passed the inspection?' she
asked as a car drew up outside.

'Yes, of course you have,' he said. 'Nice to meet you. Goodbye!'

Bethany and Chloe were getting into the car. His own car was parked nearby, and he was just in time to follow them. When Bethany's mum parked at the house he drove on, but he remembered the address – 33 Tumblers Crescent.

He drove on until he found a parking space on Bethany's road. There, he adjusted his false moustache again with a dab of glue and ruffled a little more talcum powder into his hair. He'd better keep up the disguise a bit longer. The sky was darkening, and a few fat raindrops splashed on to the windscreen.

Bethany, Mum and Chloe had hardly stepped out of the car when Bethany knew something was wrong. Sam was crying! He didn't often cry, and this was no ordinary crying – he was howling as he ran from the house, his face streaked and blotchy with tears.

'Bobby's not there!' he sobbed. 'Mum! He's gone!'

chapter 7

'Oh, Sam!' said Bethany, and put an arm round him. 'I'll help you look for him.'

'We'll talk about it inside,' said Mum, ushering them into the house. 'It's about to rain cats and dogs. In you come now.'

'He'll catch cold!' sobbed Sam. 'I have to find him.'

'Oh, sweetheart, he can't have gone far,' said Mum. 'We'll all look for him.'

'I'll take Toffee home, then I'll come and help,' offered Chloe.

Hamilton clawed his way up to the top of

Bethany's bag and peeped out cautiously –
very cautiously, because he didn't want to be
underneath any raining cats and dogs – but
soon they were all indoors. Chloe ran upstairs
to collect Toffee and hurried home, shielding
the cage with her jacket as the rain began to
fall. Dad was pulling on his wellies and anorak.

'I went to the shed to feed Bobby and
clean his cage,' said Sam, sniffing. There were
streaky stains on his face where he had
rubbed at tears with a grubby hand. 'He'd just
gone.'

'Hadn't you fastened the door catch?' asked
Mum.

'Of course I had!' said Sam. 'He'd chewed
the wood around it until it was loose, and he
got out.'

'I'll come out and look for him,' said
Bethany. 'Let me just change my shoes. Sam,
leave his cage open and put something to eat
in there in case he comes back.'

She ran upstairs to leave her bag on the bed. Hamilton peeped out at her.

'Hammy, this is an emergency,' she said. 'Sam's rabbit's escaped. I'll put you in your cage in a minute. Stay there.' Coming downstairs to find her wellies, she saw Mum at the front door talking to a man who looked familiar.

'Do you have any ID?' Mum was asking.

'I'm from the Quality Team Pet Inspection Executive,' he said, holding up the badge. 'I'm just checking up on local pet owners. Does anyone in this house have a ... say ... a hamster, for example?'

'Oh, it's you,' said Bethany, remembering how this man had pushed past her. 'You were at the pet shop.'

'Step in out of the rain for a moment,' said Mum.

Delighted and trying not to show it, Tim Taverner strode through the door. He mustn't let his excitement show on his face but, even so, Bethany wondered what he was looking so pleased about.

'We're having a bit of a pet problem,' confessed Mum.

'Really?' said Tim, sounding much too keen. 'Got a problem hamster, maybe? I could take him off your hands, if you like?'

'Certainly not!' cried Bethany.

'Oh, so you have got a hamster!' said Tim.

'Excuse *me*,' said Mum in the very firm voice that always made Bethany think she should have been a teacher, 'I don't know who you are or where you're from, but my son's rabbit has just escaped, and we all need to go and look for him.'

'Oh, what a shame,' said Tim as if it wasn't a shame at all. 'I'm not so much of a rabbit expert myself. I expect it'll turn up.'

Mum stood up very straight and put her hands on her hips. She took a step back from

Tim Taverner, not as if she were afraid, but as if she were measuring him up.

'You haven't understood the situation,' she said. 'You clearly don't care about my son's rabbit, but we do, and we're all going to look for him. That means I don't have time to talk to you about perfectly healthy pets. I've never heard of your organization – Quality Pest Executors or whoever you are – but *we* are going to find a rabbit and *you*, please, will go away. At *once.*'

She took a step towards him, and another. He had no choice but to back away, and Mum slammed the door so violently that his moustache dropped off altogether and lay on the doorstep like a large furry caterpillar.

He picked it up and retreated down the path. He was tired, cross and wet, and decided he may as well give up for today. He wasn't even sure if it was this child's hamster or the blonde one's that had the microspeck, but at least now he was getting near to it. He might as well go back to the lab to tidy everything away, write up his notes, and go home. There would be other chances to get the microspeck back, now that he had such a good lead.

Bethany kicked off her shoes, pulled on her wellies, clumped up the stairs and put her hand into her bag for Hamilton, to put him in his cage.

'Hamilton?' she said, feeling in the bag. 'Hammy? Out you come.' But there was no Hamilton.

Feeling suddenly hot and shaky with worry, she looked into the bag. There was nothing there but a chewed bus ticket and her phone, with a message on it.

GN 2 FIND BOBBY. C U SOON.

Bethany sat down and hid her face in her hands. *But he's a hamster*, she thought. *Hamsters are delicate. He'll get wet.*

And that wasn't all. Hamilton might be clever, but he'd just come from a pet shop. He had no idea about the dangers in gardens – cats, prickly bushes, ponds or simply getting lost.

Bethany felt hot tears behind her eyes. It would only have taken a few seconds to put him in his cage and lock him in! She'd meant to be such a good pet owner.

I've only just got you, she thought. *Now I've lost you already, and if you die it'll be my fault.*

Drying her eyes, she stood up. There were two animals to find now, and she wasn't at all happy about that man who called himself a pet inspector either. She put on a warm sweater – no time to get her cagoule, it was in the shed – and ran downstairs to find Chloe on the doorstep.

'I've looked in our garden and he's not there,' said Chloe. 'I can ask all the neighbours on our side if I can check their gardens too.'

'And I'll go the other way,' said Bethany. 'Text me if you find him.'

'Will do!' said Chloe, and ran down the path. Bethany stood for a moment in the rain, wishing that Hammy could feel what she was thinking – *Come back, Hamilton Hammy. You're so little. It's not safe. Come back.*

Climbing downstairs had been difficult for Hamilton, but he'd found it easy after that. Dad had left the back door open, so he had slipped out that way while Bethany and Mum had been talking on the doorstep. He'd never been out in the rain before and didn't like it a bit. There weren't any cats and dogs, but he was soon a lot wetter than was comfortable. He tried to stay under cover as he looked for Bobby, but sometimes there wasn't much in the way of shelter, and he wasn't sure if he was still in Bethany's garden or Somebody Else's. Still, he could hear her voice, so she couldn't be far away. Mum was calling to Bethany, telling her to get her cagoule out of the shed, and Bethany was insisting that she didn't need it. Hamilton ran a bit further. When he heard their voices again, they were further away than was comfortable.

Not far away, he could see a rounded stone. If he ran to that, he might be able to shelter by it while he took a good look around. He darted to the stone and found it wasn't a stone at all. He was nestling against the warm fur of a rabbit.

'Oh! Good evening!' he said in Rabbit. 'Are you Bobby?'

'Oi!' said Bobby. 'Who on earth are you?'

'I'm Hamilton, but you can call me Hammy if that's easier,' he said, feeling pleased with himself. He had never had a name before, and enjoyed using it. 'I'm Bethany's hamster.'

'Oh, I see,' said Bobby. 'Are you making a bolt for it too?'

'I beg your pardon?' asked Hamilton.

'Making a bolt,' said Bobby. 'Hightailing it. Running away.'

'Certainly not!' said Hamilton. 'What would I do that for?'

'You would, if you were me,' grumbled Bobby. 'I've had enough. I'm not going back.'

Hamilton put his head on one side while he thought about this. Bethany had kept him well fed and comfortable. There was a wheel to run on, and plenty to read so he didn't get bored. He couldn't see anything to complain about.

'What's the matter with it?' he asked. 'I'm having a great time here.'

'Does Bethany clean your cage?' asked Bobby.

'It's perfectly clean,' said Hamilton. 'It's nice and warm too, with a nest.' He was getting cold and huddled against Bobby's fur for warmth. 'Doesn't Sam clean your hutch?'

'He does when he remembers to, or when Mum and Dad remind him,' said Bobby. 'Not nearly enough.'

'Oh,' said Hamilton. He had just discovered that, as close as this, Bobby didn't smell very good. He took a step sideways.

'It's not good for a chap's health,' said Bobby. 'And my grooming's suffering. And if Sam gives me something to eat that I don't like it just stays there, going rotten. Imagine that in *your* place.'

Hamilton didn't want to imagine it at all. He could understand why Bobby was so cross, but he still didn't think running away was a very good idea.

'Still, Sam feeds you,' he said. 'What would you eat if you ran away?'

'Lots!' said Bobby. 'There's loads of free stuff growing in gardens. Grass, dandelions, vegetables, flowers – you should see the vegetables! Carrots, parsley, cabbage, all planted in rows so you can work your way along. A rabbit can help itself to all it likes.'

Hamilton had to admit that it didn't sound so bad. 'But you'd be cold at nights,' he said.

'Yes,' admitted Bobby. 'There is that.'

'And Sam really wants you back,' said Hamilton. 'I'm sure, if you gave him another chance, he'd –'

He was interrupted by Sam's voice. He was calling from somewhere in the garden.

'Bobby! Bobby!' he cried. His voice sounded high and tight, as if he were very worried and nearly crying.

'Come on, let's go home,' said Hamilton – but he realized to his dismay that Bobby wasn't moving.

Somewhere, in another garden, a dog barked. Hamilton remembered that the situation was more urgent than Bobby knew.

'Listen, Bobby,' he said. 'We can't waste time. There are cats and dogs everywhere. I heard Bethany's mum talking about it. You know what would happen to us if we ran into one of those. They're raining down from the sky!'

'What!' said Bobby.

'Tell you what,' said Hamilton, thinking quickly. 'I think I can work on Bethany and she'll talk to Sam. If you get more cleaning, will you stay?'

'Hmm,' said Bobby, looking unsure. 'OK, if you really think you can do that I might give them another chance. But just one more.'

'Great,' said Hamilton. 'Now, come with me. Get back into your cage so that Sam will find you there and think you've gone back of your own accord.' A raindrop fell from the branch of a tree and splashed on his head. 'Come on, we should hurry.'

'You're a bit clever for a little rodent, aren't you?' said Bobby, and began following

Hamilton back towards the shed. But
if Hamilton had known what was hiding
in there, he wouldn't have gone near it.

chapter 8

'Remember,' said Hamilton, shaking rain from his fur, 'when we get to the shed, go straight into your hutch and wait there.'

'Do I have to, Hammy?' said Bobby. 'It smells.'

'Then clear it out!' said Hamilton, wondering whether all rabbits were like this. 'Clear out all the dirty stuff and the rotten food. That will help Sam to see that you don't like smelly old bedding.'

Bobby stopped to scratch his ear while he thought about this.

'Oh!' he said at last. 'Oh, yes, right! Clever that!'

'And,' said Hamilton, 'when you've done that, curl up in a corner and look miserable, to make Sam feel sorry for you.'

'Like this?' said Bobby. He lowered his head and looked up with large, pleading eyes.

'That's it,' said Hamilton. 'Quick now.'

He knew they were getting nearer to the house when the family's voices became louder and clearer. He could hear Bethany's mum.

'Bethany!' Mum was calling. 'I've told you three times, you need your cagoule! It's in the shed – go and get it at once!'

'I don't need it!' Bethany called back.

'Yes, you do!' insisted Mum. 'It's rainproof!'

'Bobby!' There was a sob in Sam's voice. Bobby twitched his nose.

'There's no time to waste,' said Hamilton. 'Look, the shed door's open. I'll come with

you if you like. We'll – what did you call it –
hightail it. Run!'

They dashed for the shed and Bobby
lolloped to his hutch. Hamilton watched as
Bobby scrabbled furiously with his front paws
to clear out the dirty old sawdust, then he
turned and kicked the door shut.

'Goodbye, Bobby!' called Hamilton, and
turned to go.

For less than a second, he stood frozen with
terror. He was looking into the wide yellow
eyes of a hunting cat. It was crouched down,
ready to spring.

Don't panic, Hamilton told himself. *Think!*
The cat patted a paw towards him as if he
were a toy to play with. Hamilton hopped to
one side and the cat swiped at him with the
other paw, only just missing him. He hopped
back a little. The cat was enjoying this, and
purred. Slowly, as if it had all the time in the
world, it crept nearer to him.

Glancing up, Hamilton could see something hanging on the shed door. That must be the rainproof cagoule Bethany's mum had talked about! If he could reach it, he had a chance. It was raining cats and dogs, so this must be a rain-cat. If so, the cagoule would keep it away!

Unfortunately, the cat was still crouching between Hamilton and the cagoule, watching him with sharp eyes and, he was sure, even sharper claws. The cagoule was too high up for Hamilton to reach in a single jump, but if he could only get on top of Bobby's cage, he should be able to manage it. Hating to turn his back on the cat, but knowing that he had to, he turned and ran up the wire mesh of the cage.

The cat's claws swished behind him, and missed. Hamilton landed on the hutch, dodged one way then the other, gathered himself up for the greatest jump of his life, and leapt for the cagoule, his paws stretched out in front of him.

Just at that moment, the cat dived for him. It was so close that Hamilton could feel its breath, and knew that the sharp teeth were bared. He caught at a button on the cagoule, and dropped into a pocket, where he curled up, making himself as small as possible.

The cat stood on its hind legs, sniffing at the pocket. It patted the coat with its paws.

Hamilton stayed huddled in the pocket. He felt safe in there but, like all hamsters, he felt the cold, and he'd been cold for too long this evening. He fluffed out his fur to warm himself. *I am not frightened*, he thought. *I am cold. That's all*. All the same, he wished Bethany would come and find him. Perhaps the cat would just get bored or hungry, and go home for its dinner. He hoped so.

But the cat would not give up. Stretching

on its hind legs, it got its claws in the fabric and tugged at the cagoule.

It's all right, thought Hamilton. *Even if the cat pulls it down, I'll be all right.* And *I'm safe*, he told himself, as the cagoule began to slide on its peg. *I'll be safe so long as I stay in this pocket. Sooner or later the cat will go away.* He could feel his heart beating very hard and fast, as if something had been wound up too much.

'All right, Mum, I'm getting it!' called Bethany.

Boots squelched outside, and the door was thrown back so hard that Hamilton swung wildly in the pocket. Feeling violently seasick, he clung with his claws to the inside of the pocket as Bethany lifted the cagoule from its hook and put it on.

'I've got it, Mum!' she shouted. 'And Mrs Jennings' cat's in here! Go home, Min!' Then she gave a little shriek. 'It's Bobby! Mum, Bobby's back! Where's Sam?'

Suddenly, everyone was running. Sam was flying through the doors to pick up Bobby, Bethany's mum and dad were following, and Chloe, out of breath, had joined them. Bethany knelt by Bobby's cage. Very, very cautiously, Hamilton peeped out.

He drew back in shock. The cat's eyes were only centimetres from his own. The mouth was open in a snarl that showed long, sharp teeth . . . Then, to his great joy, he saw Dad pick up the cat firmly and say, 'Come on, Min, they'll be wondering where you are.'

'I'll take him to Mrs Jennings,' said Chloe, and took the cat in her arms.

Hamilton wriggled until he could see better. Sam was huddled on the floor beside the rabbit hutch, hugging Bobby. Bethany, who was sniffing a bit, now had both arms round Dad, occasionally letting go to wipe the back of her hand across her eyes. Sam stood up with Bobby in his arms.

'Mum, will you hold Bobby while I clean out his hutch?' he asked. 'It looks as if he's been trying to do it himself.'

Bobby, who by now was being stroked and cuddled in Mum's arms, caught Hamilton's eye. He gave a look which plainly meant *I think it's working!*

'Don't cry, Bethany,' said Dad. 'It's all right now.'

It wasn't all right, but Bethany couldn't explain that. Nobody else knew that her Hammy was missing. He could be dying of cold. The cat might have found him and she might never see him again – that thought made her cry so much that she had to sit down. She put her hand into her cagoule pocket in case there was a tissue in there. Hamilton gently bit her to let her know where he was.

'Ow!' she squeaked.

'What's the matter?' asked Mum and Dad.

'Nothing,' she said. She'd stopped crying already.

chapter 9

The first thing Bethany did, when she got upstairs, was to wrap Hamilton in a dry flannel (because the towels were too big for him) to warm and dry him as quickly as possible. Lying at the foot of her bed was a floppy cuddly dog called Wimble with a microwaveable pillow inside it. She took the pillow, warmed it in the microwave, and came back to find that Hamilton had folded the flannel neatly and was wearing it like a cloak. But the pillow was much more fun. When he had rolled on it, prodded it, jumped up and down on it and rubbed his face on it, he told Bethany all that had happened. It was a slow business, while Hamilton spelt out texts and Bethany tried to make sense of them. It took some time before Bethany could understand it all.

'It doesn't really rain cats and dogs,' she explained. 'It's just something people say. We say "raining cats and dogs" when we just mean that it's raining very hard.'

Y DON'T U JUST SAY IT'S RNING V HARD? he asked.

'It's just an expression,' she said.

Hamilton thought it was a silly one, but it wasn't worth the trouble of saying so.

THEN WHRE DID THE CT COME FRM? he asked.

'It didn't fall down from the sky!' said Bethany, and laughed. 'It belongs to Mrs Jennings, the music teacher, who lives next to Chloe. It's called Min, short for Minim. That's a kind of note. But,' she went on thoughtfully, 'if you believed it was really raining cats and dogs and still went out to find Bobby, you must be very brave.'

O, texted Hamilton, because he didn't know what else to say. Bethany picked him up and kissed him. He couldn't understand why people did that, but he was getting to like it.

'Are you warm enough now?' she asked.

YES, he texted, BT PL DON'T TAKE PILLOW AWAY.

'Do you promise not to eat it?' asked Bethany. 'It would make you very ill.'

PRMS, texted Hamilton.

'Then all we have to do now,' said Bethany, 'is get Sam to take more care over cleaning Bobby's cage. Leave it to me, Hammy, I'll see what I can do. I'll have a think about it.'

I'LL HAVE I 2, texted Hamilton. AND PL CALL ME HMLTN. It was all right for other people and animals to call him Hammy, but Bethany was different.

The next evening, after tea, Bethany carried Hamilton into Sam's room. She held him very gently in both hands.

'You can hold Hammy if you like,' she said. 'Take care, mind.'

Sam took Hamilton, who looked up at him, twitching his nose. Sam stroked his fur.

'He's very nice,' said Sam. 'Rabbits are more fun, but he's not bad for a hamster.'

Hamilton turned to Bethany with his eyes wide in indignation, looking very shocked and very lovable at the same time. Bethany smiled to reassure him.

'About Bobby,' she said to Sam, 'I was just reading somewhere – I think it was at school – something about how rabbits get very unhappy if they're not kept clean.'

Sam's expression hardened in a way she'd

often seen. It was the way he looked when he was ready to argue all evening, if necessary, that he was right and she was wrong. She went on hastily.

'The way you cleaned out his cage yesterday, when he came back,' she said, 'it looked really good. Really comfortable.'

The anger left Sam's face. 'When I found him last night he'd scraped the old bedding out,' he said. 'He was shivering in the corner with his ears down, and he looked miserable. I'm never, ever *ever* going to let him get like that again. I promised him.'

'Good,' said Bethany.

'I was always *going to* clean him out,' explained Sam. 'Every day I was going to clear out his hutch, but I always ran out of day.'

'Then you'd better always do it as soon as you get home from school,' said Bethany. 'While you've still got your coat on and before you get interested in anything else.'

'All right, don't go on,' said Sam as he handed Hamilton back to her. 'I promise, OK? But I'm not promising you. I'm promising Bobby. Promises to animals are really important because they can't look after themselves.'

'That's very true,' said Bethany.

chapter 10

At Number 38, Chloe took Toffee out of his
cage and told him all about the hunt for Bobby.
At Number 40, Minim the cat stared at the fire
and thought about that small furry animal. It
had been too big and fluffy for a mouse,
and hadn't smelt quite right. At Bethany's house,
Dad and Sam mended the hutch door and Sam
made a sign to put over it — BOBBY — and
added: HE BITES. He didn't, but Sam said it
might stop anyone from trying to steal him. He
never wanted to lose Bobby again.

★

Tim Taverner filled in his records of all the work he had done that week (or, at least, all the bits he wanted people to know about). Then he opened the diary he was keeping secret.

'Microspeck not found,' he wrote. 'No trace in shop waste. Found a link with 33 Tumblers Crescent, then lost track.'

He locked the diary away, and sniffed at his hands, then at the sleeve of his jacket. He wasn't sure if he'd quite managed to wash off the smell of pet shop and lavender.

There was a tap at the door. Mary the cleaner was there, smiling and sensible, with her Hoover and her baskets of dusters and polish.

'I won't get in your way, Dr Taverner,' she said.

'Mary,' he said as she came in, 'do I smell like a hamster cage?'

'Really, Dr Taverner!' she said. 'You don't

smell of any such thing. If anything, you smell of . . .' She sniffed. 'Lavender soap. It's like the kind my daughter uses. It's very nice.'

She looked at him again, more carefully. She hadn't noticed that his hair seemed to be going grey – but when she looked again she saw that it wasn't grey at all. There was something white and streaky in his hair. Maybe he'd had a bit of an accident with flour, or plaster of Paris, or some such thing, and the rain had made it run – no, it smelt like talcum powder. Whatever it was, it wouldn't be polite to mention it.

The fake identity badge lay on the table. The rain had got into it, making the name and the words blur, but the initials at the bottom were still clear.

'QTPIE,' she read out loud. 'Cutie Pie! Isn't that nice! Now, you go home, Dr Taverner. I know you, you always work too late.'

*Scented soap. Powder. And a badge spelling
'Cutie Pie'.* Mary thought it all over as she
cleaned the office. Perhaps Dr Taverner had a
girlfriend. Good. He needed to get out more.

Sam, who had been outside to say goodnight
to Bobby and give him fresh water, stopped to
look into Bethany's room. Bethany was
sprawled across her bed, reading. There was
no sign of Hammy, but scrabbling sounds
came from the nest box, and now and again
a bit of sawdust would fly out as if he were
digging in there. Sam watched for a while,
then decided that, if Hammy wasn't going
to do anything more interesting than that,
there was no point in staying. Hammy, he
decided, was cute but boring. Not fun and
intelligent, like Bobby.

'Goodnight,' he said.

'Goodnight, shut the door,' said Bethany.

Hamilton was extremely busy. He had seen

that Bethany's bedroom walls were decorated with pictures she'd drawn and photographs she'd taken on holiday and on school trips. This seemed like a very good idea to Hamilton, who was now scratching pictures of Bethany, an apple and a mobile phone on the wall of his nest box. Then he added one more picture, but he couldn't understand why he'd drawn that. It was a drawing of a salad baguette with sesame seeds on the top. He sat back and looked at it. He knew exactly what it was, even though he knew he'd never seen one before.

Bethany put a marker in her place in the book. 'Goodnight, Hamilton Hammy,' she said.

Night? It must be time for a run on the wheel. Hamilton finished his picture, climbed on to the wheel, adjusted its timing, and ran his fastest, as if he could run into his next adventure.

Bethany lay awake, smiling, her eyes open

in the darkness. She couldn't sleep. Here beside her, running on his wheel, was the most wonderful pet in the world. Now that Hamilton had come into her life, whatever would happen next?

She could hardly wait for tomorrow.